The Fortune
A novella

Lisa Buffaloe

The Fortune

Visit the author's website at http://lisabuffaloe.com

ISBN-13: 978-0692070536
ISBN-10: 0692070532

Cover design: Scott Buffaloe

Printed in the United States of America

The Fortune

A cryptic clue -- A setup for fun or danger?

Joy Davidson's life is root bound to the gardening center she inherited from her grandparents. Orphaned at the age of two, Joy found escape in dreaming of an adventurous life. However, her dreams seem to have left her in the dirt.

Eric West missed his family, missed the Idaho mountains, and especially missed Joy. He's returned to Boise ready to build an exciting life and has set in motion the means to make his plan succeed.

When a strange man throws a fortune cookie into Joy's lap, will the cryptic clue inside lead her and Eric to adventure or danger?

Chapter 1

Joy Davidson stared out the glass coffee shop door and spotted the lime-green, older-than-dirt, immaculate Jeep. Kristen's vehicle glowed like a neon sign; then again, everything her best friend did brought attention. Kristen exited her ride, and as usual, stopped traffic.

Men waiting in cars gawked as she walked by on long legs covered in tight jeans, high-heeled boots, and a turtleneck that hugged every curve of her curvy body.

Joy sighed as she surveyed her own somewhat-clean sweatshirt, worn jeans, and tennis shoes. When God handed out voluptuous bodies, hers wasn't on the list. Kristen had blossomed at sixteen and took all the hills which had left Joy standing in the flat prairie.

A man in a business suit bumped Joy as he hurried to open the door for Kristen.

Kristen thanked the man who stood at attention in the open doorway.

Most men didn't actually stare and drool; they'd keep their heads down or pretend to look intently at anything other than Kristen. However, out of the corner of their eyes they watched her every move. Yet, her friend remained totally oblivious to their admiration.

"Sorry, I'm late." Kristen gave Joy a quick hug and stood in line to order. "Brandon stopped me as I came out of my apartment and kept talking about the weather."

Poor Brandon, he'd lived next door to Kristen for the last year and had tried everything to get her attention. "He's probably just looking for an excuse to see you." Joy joined her friend in line and stood in Kristen's shadow.

"This time you're right, he actually asked me out this weekend."

Joy had to force her mouth not to open in shock. "He finally asked you out?" She smiled at the thought. Brandon was super nice and a great looking guy. "What did you say?"

"I told him I was leaving to work on a client's home in Sun Valley."

"Aw, poor guy."

"Yeah, he actually paled."

Joy imagined Brandon holding out his heart and watching it wither. "Would you have gone out with him?"

"Definitely. But he didn't say anything else, just kind of staggered away."

"You broke his heart."

"Oh, I hope not." Kristen put her hand on her chest. "He can ask me out when I get back. He could have asked me a year ago, and I would have gone out with him. Guys are such strange creatures, aren't they?"

Joy nodded in agreement. She hadn't figured out any of them. A few boyfriends were scattered in her background but nothing serious, and nothing that helped her decipher anything about the species called man.

A businessman in front of her stepped aside and motioned with his hand. "Please, you ladies go ahead. I'm still thinking."

They thanked him and both stepped to the counter.

Joy shook her head as the guy moved behind them and stood in the puddle of his own drool. The only one who drooled for her was her dog.

After ordering and receiving their coffee, they walked to a small table in the back.

Kristen turned to Joy. "You seem down this morning?"

"I'm okay." Joy stared out the window at a young mom holding her little girl's hand as they skipped down the sidewalk. Joy squeezed the bridge of her nose willing away any tears. Twenty-four years ago, her parents had been killed in a car wreck. Losing your family when you're only two wasn't fair. She blew out a breath and tried to think of something else. "I've just been thinking."

"Well stop that." Kristen sat straight and beamed her smile. "I've got some great news."

Joy shook off her mood and leaned forward. "What's your news?"

"Roger Thomas." Kristen sat there with a grin that said Joy should read her mind.

"The actor?"

"Yes!" Kristen's face beamed ... megawatted. "He's my client. That's who is in Sun Valley."

"The famous, latest leading-man, actor, Roger, gorgeous guy, Roger? You're going to work on his house?"

Kristen nodded. "Can you believe it? He called my office yesterday evening. I couldn't wait to tell you this morning. I'll leave soon and

Lisa Buffaloe

stay at my aunt's house. Can you come with me?"

Joy cringed at the thought. The last time she tried to help with a project, she'd wound up dropping a vase on a client's toe which just happened to be a very rich, socialite client. "No, can do. I've got to get ready for the spring rush. People are getting antsy to plant now that the snow is melting on the mountains."

"Oh, good grief, they have at least two weeks before it's safe to put things in the ground. Come on, wc'll have fun."

"I really wish I could, but I can't."

Kristen sat back and crossed her arms. "I knew you wouldn't, but we'd have so much fun together."

"You'll do great without me, especially since I can't decorate my way out of a paper bag."

"True, but we always have fun." Kristen steepled her perfectly manicured fingers. "Why are you so glum?"

"I don't know." Joy avoided her friend's gaze. "Maybe... it's because my birthday's next week."

"You shouldn't be down about that. Twenty-six is still young." Kristen grinned her mischievous grin. "I've already bought you something."

"Thank you for the gift, but I really hoped life would be different."

"I know what you mean. I thought I'd be living in Switzerland and married to a Baron."

"You've been to Europe more times than I can count."

"It's so great over there. I love the towering mountains that take your breath away." Kristen punctuated her statement with a deep breath.

Joy twirled the last remnants of her coffee. She hadn't been out of Idaho more than two times, once to visit a college friend who moved to Texas and the other to drive into Canada just to say she'd left the country. Her life was safe, boring, and downright dull.

"I'm worried about you." Kristen flipped a napkin at her. "Birthdays usually are a bright spot for you."

"It's not that. Remember growing up we had all those dreams about adventures?"

Kristen leaned forward. "Spies, baby." Her voice took on the tone of a conspirator. "Traveling the world, working with James Bond, moving secret documents through underground organizations."

"Careful, someone might be watching." Joy grinned and did a quick survey of the room.

"Don't worry; I sprayed my anti-spy spray when I stepped inside. Speaking of spies, have you seen Eric?"

Joy squelched a tiny unwelcome jump in her heartbeat. Kristen's older brother had grown way too handsome, and his chocolate brown eyes melted a place in her heart that had grown far too cold. "Yes, he stops by every few days."

Kristen leaned toward her. "And?"

"And, what?" Joy adjusted in her seat trying to stifle her smile. Eric had always been, and always would be, a good friend. Throughout the years they had kept in touch through phone calls and e-mails, but since he'd moved back to the area, something seemed different.

"He's always been interested in you, but I think you've moved up several notches."

Joy's heart did a back flip and quivered. "Eric is your brother, which kind of makes him like my brother." The thought of anything more was strange, yet oddly compelling. If Eric hadn't been so annoying during their teen years, maybe he would have been someone she would have dated. Not that he ever asked her out.

Kristen grinned. "You know, with him back in town, we could start doing crazy things like we used to. He can be our bodyguard for fun road trips. We could go camping again in the wilderness, hike mountains, white-water raft, or fly to some fun destinations."

"We can do that without him."

"True, but you gotta admit he makes things more entertaining."

"Annoying is more like it. He pestered me to death before he left for college."

"He pestered you because he loves you."

"Loves me? Ha! He tormented me." Joy let loose her smile. His torments were always enjoyable.

"That was just a sign of his affection. That's what guys do. You watch, the fun has only begun. I just know this is going to be your year. Good things are coming for both of us."

"Haven't we said the same thing every year since we graduated from high school?"

"Maybe adventure isn't what we thought." Eyes focused in the distance, Kristen sat back in her chair. "Maybe it's about being content where you live, being happy right where you are. We both create things in our own way. Maybe it's not the wild life we dreamed about, but for the most part we enjoy ourselves."

"Getting rather philosophical this morning, aren't you?"

Kristen sat straight in her chair. "You impressed? I've been reading classic literature."

"I think I liked it better when you watched cartoons."

"Tsk. Tsk. Oh, you're just grumpy because it's been gray the last week." Kristen pointed to the window, and a guy passing outside grinned big and waved. "The sun is shining and spring is coming. Pretty soon customers will be flocking in the doors buying all your little plant babies."

"Sunshine, springtime, and new growth definitely makes me happier. You need to come see some of the new peonies."

"Definitely. I was planning on having you put together a basket for me to take when I go meet Roger. My clients always love your work."

A trill signaled, and Kristen looked at her phone. "Just a sec, need to answer this text." She typed at lightning speed, her manicured nails clicking away. "Better run, but I'll stop by this evening with dinner from the Thai place."

Joy said goodbye to Kristen, then walked to the back where she'd parked. Her grandfather's truck had been bequeathed to her along with the nursery. The hand-painted Davidson's Nursery sign faded by weather and time. Maybe she'd have Kristen work her art magic and revitalize the colors.

Checking her cell phone, Joy hopped into the driver's seat. She rolled down her windows and took a deep breath of fresh air. Her cell phone signaled three missed calls, two from her buyers, one unknown. With spring officially on the calendar, orders would hopefully roll in and life would get busy.

She put her key in the ignition, and before backing out, checked over her shoulder.

A black SUV with tinted windows rolled past.

Joy chuckled to herself thinking of the earlier conversations about spies. Idaho wasn't exactly a playground for international secrets.

"Wait." A man's muffled voice came from beside her vehicle.

She leaned out her window. A young guy wearing jeans and a flannel shirt crouched next to her truck. She hit the lock button and reached to roll up the window.

He half-stood, his gaze darting to the right and left. She couldn't tell if he was scared or goofy.

"Wait. I'm not going to hurt you. Take this." With a flick of his wrist, he tossed in a fortune cookie which landed in her lap. "You'll know what needs to be done."

"Seriously? A cookie?" Joy followed the mystery man's gaze behind them. "What do you mean?"

The black SUV backed up, rolled to a stop, and parked two spaces away. Tinted windows blocked her view to see inside.

Cookie guy turned and ran.

The back doors to the SUV opened. Two men wearing dark business suits and sunglasses took chase after mystery man.

Joy grabbed her phone as she rolled up her window. Should she call 911? And say what? *Help police, a strange man threw a cookie in my truck?* She could just imagine the reply, "And how old are you little girl?"

The SUV backed out and maneuvered behind her, blocking her exit. She couldn't even see through the front window. Who tinted front windows?

Way too creepy. Joy stared at the cookie. Should she eat the evidence? She speed-dialed Kristen. The phone went straight to voice mail.

The mystery vehicle crept away, paused before turning the corner, then drove down the street.

What was she supposed to do? She couldn't call the police and say she *might* have seen a crime?

Joy looked for anyone who might have seen what happened. No people in the back lot, no windows in back of the shop, and the guy and the suit-creeps were nowhere to be seen. Too weird.

Maybe one of the hidden camera things set her up and everybody was hiding in the coffee shop laughing hysterically.

She'd check with Mr. Dixon when she got back to the garden center. His early years in the military might be helpful. He always told her to pay attention to her surroundings. Why didn't she look for the license plate of the SUV?

Wait a minute. What was in the cookie? She double-checked the doors.

The cookie sat on the seat next to her. A tiny piece of paper stuck out of the end.

Without breaking the cookie, she pulled out the paper and stared at the writing.

On one side, "Fortune waits" on the other in gold pen were handwritten numbers ... 43.8262 N, 115.8325 W

Lisa Buffaloe

Chapter 2

Without checking caller ID, Eric West answered his cell phone, "Solid Rock Builders." He smiled at the information given on the other end of the line. "No problems, right? ... Good. Tell the guys I owe them. Will you be able to make the next delivery? ... Good."

He ended the call and completed a walk-through of his three homes under construction -- one a spec house, the other two built for business executives. Eric nodded to the workmen on the job site.

The time he'd spent learning the latest environment friendly building techniques were now being incorporated into the business his dad owned. The business that one day would be his.

The sound of heavy equipment preparing the lot to his right brought him back to the day's duties. Eric turned and walked down the street to his personal property overlooking Boise.

Here he would one day build his home.

The view was perfect with Table Rock's cross in the distance to the left, the old quarry, and botanical gardens below, and hiking trails meandering up the hill.

He'd always hoped and prayed one day he could return and raise a family. And, if all his hard work paid off, Joy would be part of that family. He just hoped the plans he had set into motion wouldn't drive her away but bring her into his arms.

~~~~

Joy parked in the back lot at the garden center next to Mr. Dixon's Ford F350. She greeted the other employees already hard at work. Most had been with her grandfather for twenty years before his passing.

Her dog, Barkley, came running and about knocked her down as he thumped his big Siberian husky/German Shepherd paws on her shoulders. Barkley was all teeth and wags, but his booming bark and protectiveness kept strangers at bay.

Sasha, the resident cat, sauntered over and surveyed them both. Sasha rubbed against Barkley and Joy then wandered off to survey

Lisa Buffaloe

her kingdom.

Mr. Dixon, watering the trees and humming some unknown tune, glanced Joy's way. "Plants are coming along nicely. This year will be a good one."

"I hope so." She stopped next to him. "Can I ask you something?"

"Always." Although in his late seventies, his military training showed by his posture. He continued to be a tower of strength in her daily life and times of trouble. She didn't know what she would have done without him, especially since he had stepped in as business manager and mentor when her grandparents passed away.

"I met Kristen at the coffee shop, and when I went out to the truck a guy threw this in my window." Joy held up the fortune cookie. "Then he raced off, chased by two guys in business suits from a black SUV with tinted windows. He said I would know what needed to be done."

"He didn't hurt you, did he?" Mr. Dixon turned to face her, raising one of his silver eyebrows.

"No, I'm okay. Just kind of weirded out. Should I call the police?"

He sat the hose down and stroked his chin.

"I'll call Ray and see what he thinks."

Thank goodness, Mr. Dixon's son, Ray worked at the police department. "Would you?"

Mr. Dixon nodded. "So, what was in the cookie?"

Joy handed him the piece of paper.

He studied the object for a moment. "Looks like you've been given a clue."

"A clue to what?"

"These are coordinates to a location."

"That's kind of creepy isn't it?"

"What's creepy, dear?" Her great-aunt, Willamena, floppy hat flapping, toddled over. The Grandplantmom was always a step behind conversations, probably because she talked to plants, and anyone, and everything, that would listen. As a result, people and flora alike seemed to flourish in her presence.

Joy explained the story again.

"Oh dear. I don't think you should pursue this adventure." Willamena cocked her head, her bright pink garden gloved finger tapping her chin and leaving a spot of dirt. The tapping stopped and she pointed at Joy. "Unless of course, it's something fun. Then, I think if it's something fun, you should go and do it. And speaking of fun, when are you joining my quilting group?"

At least her aunt wasn't worried about the cookie clue. "Maybe I'll come next month." Joy hugged her strong but sweet, gentle fluff-aunt.

Mr. Dixon cleared his throat. "Sorry to break up the hug fest." He smiled at Willamena who promptly blushed and even fluttered her eyelashes at him.

Red-faced, he grinned like a little kid. After a lingering sweet look, he redirected his attention back to Joy. "Do you have map program on your computer? Maybe we should check out where the coordinates lead."

A truck from one of her suppliers pulled around to the back and lurched to a stop. An unfamiliar man hopped out and walked toward them.

Barkley stood rigid, watching.

Willamena toddled toward him, "Hello, young man. You must be new."

He nodded, adjusted his worn baseball cap, glanced at each of them, his dark gaze lingering on Joy. "Just started this week. Where do you want the mulch shipment?"

Mr. Dixon moved forward. Willamena cut him off. "I can help you." She took the guy by the arm and guided him away as another male employee rushed over to help.

Barkley let out a low growl/woof.

Joy patted his head and leaned down. "My sentiments exactly." Not sure what it was about the guy, but he made her uncomfortable.

A few minutes later, she pulled her chair up to her computer desk as the satellite image zeroed in on Idaho City. Joy imagined the clue leading to some lost gold mine in the mountains.

Mr. Dixon studied the screen. "Doesn't look like a coincidence with the saying on the fortune and the location. If you go on a search, take a man with you to keep you safe."

"So, you want to go on a road trip?"

"You probably should take someone younger. Not sure I'd be much good if you have to do any hiking." He took his cell phone out of his ragged back jeans pocket. "I'll let you know what Ray says."

Even when his bad leg, Mr. Dixon could probably damage anyone with evil motives. If she took Kristen, her bombshell body would attract too much attention.

Who else could she take? The only guys she knew had families or other obligations. Then again, Eric was back in town. Maybe he'd go. Of course, he'd probably give her a hard time for following up on a fortune cookie, and

Lisa Buffaloe

the thought of spending time alone with Eric made her pulse jump about eighty notches. She shook off the emotion. He was just a friend.

Mr. Dixon handed her the phone. "Ray wants to talk to you."

Ray asked several questions, and Joy relayed as much as she could remember. He was quiet for a moment. "I'll log in what happened. Or, you can come in and file a report of suspicious activity. That would give you more to work with because the event would be recorded in more detail. We can go over the vehicle and physical descriptions of all those involved, and with a record in the system this could possibly be accessed by other government entities. Did you sense you were in any danger?"

Joy was still trying to formulate what Ray said and what kind of descriptions she could give. "Danger? Yes and no." More excitement than danger. More like a grown-up version of what she and Kristen used to play on her swing set.

"Tell you what," Ray said. "I'll come by later this evening and you can fill me in. Until then, pay attention to your surroundings. Personally, I think it's a hoax, but we want you safe."

The Fortune

She thanked him and handed the cell to Mr. Dixon. He turned his back as he listened and spoke in low tones.

Now she was really starting to worry. What if she had something those men wanted? What did the guy mean that she would know what to do? Would the other men have seen the sign on her truck? Thank goodness, the logo had faded.

Maybe she'd get the truck repainted and cut her hair. Good grief, she didn't want to live a paranoid life. Why was she worried about a fortune cookie? Her plants needed her. Flower babies sprouted all over the property. Besides that, she could thwack anyone with a shovel who gave her trouble.

"How about you stay close the next few days?" Mr. Dixon addressed her as he placed his phone back in his pocket. "Make sure you keep Barkley with you too."

Barkley sat tall and proud. He looked at Mr. Dixon then at her. She'd swear the dog understood the human language.

"I'll take care of things around here." He nodded toward the greenhouses. "Like I said, it's going to be a good year." Singing a country tune, he limped away.

Joy went to the computer and typed in Idaho City in the search engine. She'd been there several times, once to explore, another time to pan for gold in the old mining town. Even though in the 1800's the Boise Basin produced more gold than all of Alaska, she had only come home with one tiny flake. Shame her clue wouldn't lead her to a nice, watermelon-sized nugget.

She scrounged around for a baggie to place the cookie and fortune for safeguarding. Perhaps Ray would want to check it out.

Maybe she shouldn't have touched anything without gloves. Then again, could they dust a cookie for fingerprints?

She needed to think. She needed to dig.

Two hours later, Joy stood and wiped her hands on her already muddy jeans. The hole she'd dug wasn't exactly all the way to China, but she did make progress.

Maybe baking all those mud pies when she'd been a little girl bonded her to the earth. Her family roots were here, and outside digging in the dirt had always been a source of comfort.

Nothing matched planting a seed and watching it grow, tending and nurturing plants to their full potential.

Sprawled on his side, Barkley lay at her feet. Paws twitching and tail thumping against the ground, he ran in his dreams, perhaps chasing a squirrel or playing his favorite game of fetch. She'd love that kind of freedom.

Digging taxed her muscles and released tension that crept up her shoulders, that gargoyle-like heaviness that tried, and many times succeeded, to bring her down. Her digging helped her relax, but she never could dig out the hollow place in her chest.

Her grandparents had given her a loving home, but now they were all gone. To add to the frustration, the memories of her parents lived more in photos than in her mind. She could imagine how happy they would have been together. How happy they *should* have been together.

Joy's teeth jarred when her shovel struck a rock. She dug further trying to find the edges. The thing was huge. Placing the shovel on one end of the stone, she used all her strength and attempted to dislodge Boulderzilla. The rock wouldn't budge. Ugh.

Any project always took twice as long as expected since the ground around Boise consisted more of rocks than dirt.

She surveyed what she had unearthed. Dynamite might come in handy. Shame they didn't package tiny TNT.

"Hey."

At the sound of Eric's voice, Joy's heart jumped. Part of her wanted to dive inside the hole and hide, and the other part of her wanted to leap into his arms.

Eric crouched next to her self-made sinkhole and rubbed Barkley's fur. "Now that I'm back, I'll be glad to work anytime you have a job this big."

"Some things have to be done alone." She rubbed her palms together hoping to remove at least the top layer of grime.

Eric nodded and offered his hand. "Need help getting out of the pit?"

For some reason, Eric always knew when something was troubling her. Maybe her tell-tale digging gave her away. When younger, her backyard looked like attack of the human gophers.

With Eric's rough, but gentle touch, he grabbed her hand and pulled her up. The movement brought her way too close. Close enough she could smell his cologne. Close enough to notice that cute dimple on his right cheek.

Way too close.

Joy stepped to the side and rubbed her hands again on her dirty jeans. An ache twisted in her chest. Even though she kept telling

23

The Fortune

herself nothing was between them, she missed Eric while he was in California. Since his return, he'd stopped by almost every day. She wanted him to see her as a confident woman; instead her insecurities showed. And, just like in the past, Eric rescued her from another hole she'd dug.

Eric hopped in the crater and in just a few minutes had popped the huge rock out of the ground.

Joy crossed her arms and stared at her shoes. She didn't want to be needy, but she wanted to need him, and didn't want to need him, and in a way really did need him. Ugh. She was an absolute mess.

"I've been thinking about you today." He stood next to her, tilted and dipped his head to catch her attention. "Want to talk about it?"

From the look in his eyes, he remembered the anniversary of her parent's death. Subject change was absolutely vital before she got all weepy, wimpy, or threw herself in his arms.

She turned and walked slow enough he could catch up.

Eric matched her stride, and without saying a word walked next to her.

When Joy could find her voice, she changed the subject by telling him about the

Lisa Buffaloe

coffee shop incident.

With a frown on his face, he opened the office door for her. "I don't like it."

"I'm not sure what to think." Joy sat in her desk chair while Eric propped on the edge of her desk.

Man, she was tired. Emotionally drained. Brain drained. Just drained.

Eric scratched behind Barkley's ears. "Then again, I wouldn't take seriously a clue in a fortune cookie. This morning I had a message in my breakfast cereal which read ooooooo."

Joy glared at him. "Well I think it's serious, whether you do or not. I'm driving up to Idaho City to see if I can find something."

"That's not a good idea." He stood up, crossed his arms. "At best, it's a waste of time. And at worst ... don't put yourself in a situation that isn't safe, and don't go alone."

"I can bring Barkley."

Barkley responded with a wag and nudged her leg.

"No." Eric's voice took on a forceful tone.

"I'll go with you. Just let me know, and I'll work you in my schedule."

"I can take care of myself, you know." Joy turned to face Eric. She was a big girl. "I've done just fine without you." Her cheeks grew warm as she stared into his eyes. She couldn't let down the guard around her heart. Shouldn't, couldn't, ever, take another chance at losing someone else she loved.

Eric stood and stared out the window. "I know." His voice quiet, pensive. He turned back to her, his eyes searching hers. "I want to help. Anything you need done around here? Can I take you to get some dinner?"

"No, Kristen is coming over. She's bringing Thai food."

Eric pulled out his cell phone and speed dialed. "Hey, can you bring me the usual? Thanks." He put it back in his pocket and smiled. "Caught her as she placed the order." He rested his hand on her shoulder. "Wow, your shoulders are tight."

Before she could object, he moved her long hair and started kneading his magic fingers into her sore muscles. Everything in her longed for his touch, yet tensed, and she squirmed in a half-hearted way to get him to stop.

"Be still." His hands pressed down on her shoulders. "You need this." He massaged her back. "You need to get out and play more often."

She forced herself to relax. As she submitted to his touch, she almost slumped over and drooled. "Maybe I do play."

His rubbing stopped and his breath was warm against her ear. "You work all the time."

It took her several swallows before she could reply and not drool. "I take off Sundays."

"True, but do you do anything for fun?" His fingers began to work again.

Melting.

Melting as he worked against her sore muscles.

It took her several minutes for her overly relaxed brain to engage and respond to his question. "I get to play in the dirt six out of seven days. I watch plants grow. I get to teach people how to care for nature. I wake up every day and step into a world of flowers and beautiful things."

"I meant, do you do anything outside of work?"

"I do fun things with Kristen."

Again, he stopped and leaned forward. So close she could smell his minty breath. "Joy, what do you do for you?"

Joy couldn't reply. Eric's comment hit home. She didn't have a life outside of work. Not that she didn't want something else to do, but her opportunities to meet people were limited by obligations with the business.

Shame she couldn't grow the perfect man from a seedling.

However, the perfect man she would grow would be the very man who rubbed her shoulders.

Chapter 3

Eric straightened and stepped back. If he had waited another millisecond, he would have done something wonderful and incredibly stupid like plant a kiss on Joy's beautiful mouth.

She looked up at him with those trusting, gorgeous green eyes of hers. Did she still see him like a big brother? The thought made him want to dig his own hole.

"Food time." Kristen walked in the door and lifted up two sacks. "Anybody hungry?"

Joy clambered to her feet and gave him a look he couldn't decipher.

Was she upset with him? Or did she wish he had kissed her?

Why didn't women have a little bubble over their heads that told their thoughts? Then again, maybe he didn't want to know.

"I better wash up." Joy hurried out the door before Eric could blink.

Kristen faced him. "Did you do something

to upset her?"

"I don't think so. I found her digging a hole out back."

"Oh." She cleared off the table and placed the take-out containers in a neat row. "So, what happened?"

Not sure what to say, he shrugged.

Kristen put her hands on her hips. "You did do something."

"I did not. I rubbed her shoulders."

"Oh." She gave him one of those looks. Those looks that make men wonder what women think.

"Joy's shoulders were tense. Probably because today is the anniversary of her parent's death." Eric opened the bags but didn't look at the food.

"Oh. no." Kristen plopped in the office chair and hung her head. "I should have said something this morning. I'm a horrible friend. I was so busy talking about my trip to Sun Valley, I didn't even mention it. I've got to think of something to make it up to her." She pointed a finger at his face. "Wait a minute, were you coming on to her when she's vulnerable?"

"I was trying to help."

"Oh." This time Kristen's look morphed to one like his mother used to give him. One that

Lisa Buffaloe

said she was irritated and yet not irritated.

He fought the urge to wring her neck. "Translation please?"

Kristen peeked out the door and then looked back at him. "Uh, it's sort of kind of possible ... she might know you like her."

"Why, what did you say?"

"Just that she had gone up a few notches in how you viewed her."

"Notches? What does that mean?"

"It means you find her attractive. You do, don't you?"

"I always have." He didn't mean to voice that so quickly, but it was true. Joy had a beauty that turned heads, but she never noticed. She was the perfect combination of beauty, brains, and fun.

"Always?" Kristen grinned.

"You've always what?" Joy stood in the doorway and blinked at Eric. Her head did that little cute tilt thing that made his chest ache in good ways.

Heat raced up Eric's neck. "You know, always loved living here. Always loved being with friends and family. Always loved eating Thai food." Eric grabbed and crammed a spring roll into his mouth before he stammered out anything else.

"Well, I always love being with you guys." Joy picked up a plate and smiled at them both, but just for a moment her eyes locked with his.

He grinned and would have paid a million bucks to know what she was trying to tell him— back away bucko or kiss me fool.

"Did Eric tell you what happened?" Joy's voice was low and quiet as she stood next to Kristen.

He choked. Gagged. Maybe he really did kiss her.

"Are you okay?" Joy looked like she was ready to give him the Heimlich maneuver.

He held out his hand. "Fine," he croaked.

Kristen looked at Eric like he was a frog, then back at Joy. "Tell me about what?"

Joy glanced again at Eric.

"Something happened?" Kristen glared at Eric before turning her attention back to Joy. "Are you okay?"

"Yes, I'm fine. But when I got in the truck after you left, this guy came up and tossed a fortune cookie in my car. Then he ran off because two guys in business suits from a black SUV chased him."

Kristen's perfectly brows rose. "What? A fortune cookie? Guys in a black SUV?" She shook her head and grinned. "Wait a minute, this is a setup, right? You want to play spies again?"

"Really, it happened." Joy opened her file drawer and took out a bag. "Here's the evidence."

Kristen studied the cookie. "That's bizarre. How many grown men throw fortune cookies in someone's truck window?"

"You had a guy give you a fortune cookie last year."

Kristen cringed and held up her hands in front of her. "Yes, but that was weird Walter trying to propose. I wouldn't go out with him if he was the last man on earth." She pointed to Joy's cookie. "What does it say?"

"One side says, fortune waits for those who search, and the other are coordinates to Idaho City."

"Idaho City? Maybe there is gold waiting. I hate I have to leave in the morning. You need to go check this out." Kristen pointed at Eric. "You're going with her, right?"

"She's not going." He couldn't stand the thought of something happening to her.

Joy stood next to him, pulling her full height to the level of his chest. "I am too! Somebody said I never did things for fun. So, I'm going to go have fun."

How could one woman be so frustrating and incredibly cute at the same time? "Fine. Then I'm going with you." He took his car keys out of his pocket. "You ready?"

Kristen wormed her way between them and pushed Joy and Eric apart. "Wait a minute, both of you. I brought dinner, and nobody is going anywhere tonight."

"Fine." Joy turned and rummaged through one of the bags containing the food.

"Fine." Eric reached over her and snatched the other bag before he carried her off into the sunset. He'd do anything to make sure Joy was safe, and he would follow her anywhere she let him.

~~~~

Joy savored her last bite and smiled at her friends. Everything felt good and right with the three of them back together, yet Eric's question nagged at her.

She really didn't do much of anything just for herself. Business was her life. Some days that wasn't a bad thing, other days she found a hole to dig.

Shame Eric and Kristen couldn't just move in with her and they could become their own family. Even if Eric was irritating and frustrating ... and wonderfully handsome and he smelled so good. Oh man, she was in trouble.

He stood and threw his paper plate in the trash, then turned to Joy. "What can I do to help?"

Kiss me, hold me, take me away. Oh, good grief, she was pathetic. She should have gone off by herself tonight instead of being such an emotional mess for the whole world to see. To distract herself, Joy swiped away the crumbs remaining on her desk. "Maybe set up everything for the kid's class tomorrow."

"Ah, the dirt worms. Nothing like munchkins and mud. You guys still doing that every week?"

"Yep. We had an abundance of Jade plants and little flowers, so we're letting the kids plant their own."

"Great. Tell me what to do, and I'm your man."

Joy leaned back in her chair. Eric had said that line since he was ten.

And, now he really was a man. A mighty fine man. But would he ever be *her* man?

Whoa.

She opened her desk drawer and peered inside at something, anything other than looking at how nice looking he was, and thinking how nice it was to have him back in town and staring at those dark eyes of his that stayed so full of light.

He probably still saw her like a little sister. If she wasn't so tired, she'd go dig another hole.

Kristen cleaned off the table. "I'm ready to help too." She removed designer gardening gloves from her purse and tugged them on her manicured fingers.

Joy considered sitting on her hands. As much as she loved Kristen, insecurities came out in abundance when they were together.

Barkley, ears perked, hurried to the door and stood at attention.

"Joy?" Ray's voice came from outside.

She called Barkley to her side. He responded with a wag, sat next to her, and kept a sharp eye on Ray as he entered her office.

Ray surveyed each of them. His police gaze measuring, taking in details.

"Did I come at a bad time?" Ray said.

"Nope." She pointed to her friends. "You remember Eric and Kristen?"

"Definitely, good to see you both." Ray nodded and exchanged handshakes.

An awkward silence planted itself in the room. Joy gazed at Eric's questioning eyes.

"Ray dropped by to talk about the fortune cookie incident."

Kristen grabbed Eric's arm and pushed him toward the door. "We'll go set up everything for the kid's class tomorrow."

After they left, Ray moved over a chair and sat next to Joy. "Tell me everything that happened."

~~~~

Eric wished he was closer to the office to hear what Joy told Ray. He knew Ray was a friend, but still ... maybe Joy didn't tell him everything since she called the police.

And, why did she fight him about going with her? They'd been friends forever, but was she wanting to move on without him? Start a new life? The thought made him sick.

Needing a distraction, he arranged the planting cups into a smiley face on the kids table. Eric stepped back and addressed Kristen. "What do you think?"

She grinned and shook her head. "Cute. But what do you think about this fortune thing?"

"I don't like it."

"Me neither. It gives me the willies."

Kristen set the kid-size planting tools next to each seat. "Wait a minute. Did you do this to get some time alone with her?"

"Why didn't I think of that? Set up an adventure to do some fun road trips together. Interesting idea."

"Did you?"

"I wish I had for several reasons." Eric avoided Kristen's penetrating look. "Do you have any thoughts?"

"Spy stuff at ten was fun, but now it just seems creepy to think someone might be out there watching her." Kristen perched on the edge of the small table and surveyed him.

They both stopped and looked around the garden center. Most of the employees they remembered since they were kids. All seemed harmless.

Did someone who knew Joy play a fun gag or did it involve danger?

Kristen rubbed her hands across her arms. "Maybe someone is trying to get Joy by herself."

"I hope this is a hoax. Cause if it's not, I'd camp out in her den if she would let me."

Kristen stood and paced. "Should I stay here instead of going to Sun Valley?"

"No, you need to take care of your

business obligations. I'll be here."

"You promise to keep her safe?"

Eric nodded. "I promise." He'd do anything to make sure Joy was safe.

"Hey guys." Joy walked up and smiled at Eric's creativity. "Cute."

Kristen grabbed Joy's arm. "What did Ray say?"

Joy leaned against the table. "Well, we're hoping it wasn't anything weird. Are you guy's familiar with letterboxing?"

Eric boxed at the air. "I prefer sparring with e-mail."

Joy punched his arm. "No. It's where you find things based on GPS locations."

"I've heard of that." Kristen rearranged the cups on the table. "Somebody was talking about it last year, maybe it was Brandon. You travel all over the place finding these small weatherproof boxes. Sounded like fun."

"Well, maybe this is just something like that."

Eric moved closer to her. "I still don't like it."

"Well, then you can come with me when I drive up and look." Joy's grin dared him to comment.

He puffed his chest. "I'll report for

bodyguard duty anytime you need me."

~~~~

Joy locked the back door of her house and tossed off her shoes. Barkley padded past her and went straight to his food in the kitchen.

Besides the sad anniversary, hole digging, and weird fortune cookie thing, her day had been good. Eric and Kristen's friendship meant more than they would ever know.

Eric did seem interested, maybe, or did she just hope he was interested? He'd walked her to her door after they finished preparing for the children. He had kept his distance, either being respectable because Kristen was watching, or maybe he wasn't interested. Good grief, if only she could put her brain on pause and just enjoy life without overthinking.

Tonight, a bubble bath sounded like a great idea. Maybe she'd even start a new book she downloaded. Willamena had her hooked on nineteenth century clean, Christian romances.

After grabbing the e-reader off the coffee table, Joy walked to the front door and checked the locks, all were secure. Now, her soaking tub called.

An hour later, swathed in a blanket of

fading bubbles, Joy added more hot water to her now tepid bath. Her books gave her a chance to play and escape.

As Barkley snored on the floor next to the tub, Joy turned back to her book and immersed herself in her heroine's adventure.

Sinking deeper in the water, Joy smiled at the thought of authoring her own story. If she could pen her own life, she'd be a sexy, brave, super-smart woman who could fight crime and save the world. And, of course, she would need a handsome partner on her escapades. Eric's face came to mind.

A bubble hovered and lit on her arm. With a quiver, it popped and disappeared. Eric would be like all the other things she had wanted, nothing in her life stayed.

Barkley growled and jumped up, his ears cocked toward the other room.

"What is it, boy?"

He pawed at the door to get out.

Goosebumps pebbled on her arms. Joy flipped the drain plug, grabbed her robe, and opened the bathroom door.

Barking like a mad dog, Barkley tore through the bathroom, rocketed down the hall and bashed against the front door. His growl and furious bark shot up every hair on her neck.

Still growling, he stood his ground, face forward, fur spiked, his dog odor reaching new heights.

Whatever, or whoever, was outside was not friendly. Ears plastered to his head, Barkley looked back at her. She'd swear if he talked, he would be telling her to keep her distance.

Joy ran for her cell phone and speed-dialed Eric's number.

Right now, she needed a bodyguard.

Chapter 4

Eric stomped on the brakes and lunged out of his car. If anyone hurt Joy, he would personally tear off their arms.

He did a quick study of the area and hurried to the front porch.

He banged on the door. "Joy, it's me!" If anyone was around they would know he was coming, and he meant business.

Barkley's frantic barking made Eric want to chainsaw through the door. With Joy living alone, he had to get a key. He needed to be here for her.

The door flew open, and Joy in a fuzzy pink bathrobe ran to his arms. "I was so scared."

Eric pulled her trembling body close. "I'm here. Everything's okay."

Big old, Barkley whimpered at his feet, his tail wagging slow and low. Man, they were both scared to death.

"What happened?" He took a deep breath

reveling in the smell of her damp, clean hair.

"I don't know. Barkley's never barked like that." Joy's voice was an octave higher than normal and her teeth actually chattered.

She pointed at the big dog, "He ran to the door and just about would have torn it down if he could have." She clung tighter to him, her face buried in his chest. "Did you see anything?"

Eric again scanned the area in the darkening twilight. Nothing seemed out of place. "I'll check the area. And, I'm staying tonight."

Joy pulled away, her head down. "You can't stay."

"I can't?"

She did a nervous glance around her yard and back toward the gardening center. "I mean it wouldn't be proper."

"Proper? We practically grew up together. What isn't proper about me sleeping on your couch?"

Joy motioned him inside, then closed and locked the door behind her. "I mean, Willamena and Mr. Dixon, what would they think?"

"They probably would be glad I stayed to keep you safe."

"But your car would be here in the morning. Or, they would see you leaving and then everyone would think we slept together."

"Slept together? Where is this coming from?"

Joy hugged her arms across her chest and slumped against the wall. "I don't know. I'm scared, and I don't want to be alone. I'll call Willamena to stay with me."

"Willamena? What would she do? Hit a bad guy with a purse?"

"Her purse is really big."

"Joy, you're not thinking right."

"I know." She shook her head and walked to the couch. "But I don't know what to do."

She sat down and pulled a blanket on top of her. "I don't want you to go." Her voice came out barely a whisper.

"I'll stay here on the couch." He sat next to her. "You can even lock your bedroom door. Plus, you've got Barkley."

"What will people think?"

"Do I need to call Mr. Dixon, Willamena, and make a public announcement to every employee at the garden center that I am only staying to keep you safe?"

Joy nodded but didn't look at him. "That would probably be good, but no one would believe us."

"What?" Eric tried to regain control. His voice had taken on a tone he knew it shouldn't. His head about to explode from a discussion that made no sense.

Joy glanced toward the door. "Maybe we should call Kristen."

"Kristen is packing to go to Sun Valley."

"She could bring her suitcase and stay here with us. Then it would be okay."

Eric stared at Barkley who looked as confused as he felt. "Let me get this straight. I can stay here as long as someone else is here?"

"Yes. But maybe you should go to Kristen's and get her car so no one sees you here in the morning."

Eric shook his head. "This isn't the 1800's."

If she felt the same way about him he did about her, he'd grab her and carry her off to the wedding chapel and no one would care about anything. Instead, he blew out a breath and sunk back on the couch.

~~~~

Joy pulled her legs up under her and made sure she was properly covered. She was such an idiot. Scared to death, and she still couldn't be honest with her feelings. Right now, her thoughts weren't in line with what she was telling Eric. In his arms everything felt right and safe, and she wished he would just stay forever. Unfortunately, now all he seemed was irritated.

Maybe she'd read too many historical novels. Life in the twenty-first century was radically different than back then. But how do you maintain being a lady when you need someone to keep you safe? Even Barkley seemed scared, and Barkley was *never* scared.

Eric stood. "Tell you what, I'll take a flashlight and go with Barkley, and we'll check around the house. You stay inside locked up and safe, and when I return we'll talk about options." He smiled and placed his hand on her cheek. "It's going to be okay."

Tears threatened to make their way past her lashes. She closed her eyes and rested her face against his warm fingers. "I'm sorry about all of this."

He knelt in front of her. "Hey, I'm always here for you. That's what friends are for."

Now she really wanted to cry.

She didn't want to be just friends.

~~~~

Eric muttered to himself as he checked around the house. He had missed his chance to tell Joy how he felt. Instead he had said that's what friends are for. *Friends?* He wanted to move beyond friendship.

Barkley stayed close and still seemed nervous. Eric checked the ground, no footprints, and nothing seemed to be disturbed. He was clueless as to what had scared them.

A sound up the hill perked Barkley and Eric's ears. Barkley let out a deep growl and focused his attention toward the main road.

Eric switched off his flashlight, kept one hand on Barkley's collar, and moved through the shadows.

Male voices came from outside the house around the corner.

Barkley tugged forward. Eric prayed the big dog wouldn't bolt or give them away before he figured out what was going on.

Two guys were deep in conversation, neither probably much older than sixteen.

Eric shook his head and let out a sigh as he listened to their discussion. The boys had misread directions to a friend's house and were talking on their cell phones to figure out how to find their way. Evidently, they had visited several homes in search of their buddy.

Lisa Buffaloe

Even Barkley seemed to understand. His tail went up and a spring returned in his step as they turned back toward home.

Eric had mixed emotions about reporting back what they discovered. Having Joy rush into his arms sure had been nice, and keeping watch over her all night would have been even nicer.

~~~~

Joy sat on the couch and tried to catch her breath. While Eric was gone she had combed her hair, changed into jeans and a shirt, and called Kristen, who was now on her way.

While folding the afghan, Joy wondered how on earth she'd turned into a whining, needy woman. Maybe she lacked some major vitamin, like chocolate.

Then again, being a helpless female definitely had its perks when it came to being in Eric's strong arms.

Her fear had dissipated, but still the anxiety about Eric remained. Joy fell back on the couch and stared at the ceiling. "A little help from above sure would be nice. Could you help with this whole situation? Maybe give me a sign about Eric? Let me know if I should pursue him or not?"

Silence as usual.

She and God hadn't talked much since her grandparents passed. Sure, she continued attending church, but the distance seemed insurmountable. Whether God liked it or not, she was still mad he took her parents and then her grandparents.

Joy wondered if sometimes God was just waiting for her to talk it out with him. But, letting out her real feelings didn't seem intelligent. Then again, didn't God already know her thoughts? Her *every* thought?

Uh oh, that meant she was in trouble—big trouble.

A knock sent her scurrying to look through the peephole. Eric stood outside. With a relieved sigh, she unlocked the deadbolt and opened the door.

With a big smile on his face, he held out his arms.

Even though she was tempted to throw herself back in the safety of his embrace, she stood her ground.

Eric sighed and dropped his hands. "I was hoping for a repeat performance."

Joy outwardly ignored his comment, but her heart whimpered. "Did you find anything?"

"Would you believe a big, grizzly bear?"

"No. But by the look on your face, I think you discovered the reason for Barkley's earlier behavior." She moved to the side as he and Barkley entered.

"Yeah, a couple of teenagers were lost and looking for a buddy's house." Eric locked the door and turned back to her. "I think you're safe for the night. However, I'll be glad to stay if you need me."

"I called Kristen."

"So, that makes it safe for me to stay, right?" He puffed up his chest and took a military stance. "You always need a bodyguard. Never can be too careful."

"Eric, thank you for coming over. I'm sorry about ruining any plans you had for the evening."

"I can't think of a better way to spend my time." He held out his hands in apology. "Not the things that scared you. I mean ... I always like seeing you." His grin reminded her of when they were younger.

"Really?" Heat ignited from head to toe at the sweet look he gave her. "I mean, thanks."

He moved toward her, close enough she could feel his warm breath. His gaze rested on her lips.

Every nerve ending in Joy's body went on high alert. He wanted to kiss her? *Really?* Internally she squealed with glee. Maybe God did hear her prayer. Joy leaned toward him, her lips just itching for that sweet connection.

The doorbell chime made her heart lunge to her throat. For the first time in her life, Joy wished her friend hadn't been quite so available.

Eric's lips grazed her forehead. "I guess that's Kristen."

"Probably." Delightfully woozy, Joy moved closer.

Kristen knocked and called to her from the other side of the door.

Joy stared at Eric's handsome face. "I guess I should answer."

"Probably." His arms came around her and pulled her closer.

Kristen continued knocking, her voice growing in volume.

Joy could stay here forever, safe in Eric's arms.

Throwing away cautious thoughts mumbling her brain, Joy planted a kiss on Eric's lips.

Lisa Buffaloe

Chapter 5

The morning sun warming her back, Joy still found her legs a touch wobbly after last night's kiss. She surveyed the nursery. This morning colors seemed more vibrant.

Kissing Eric was all so weird, wild, and wonderful. He had seen her at her worst and still wanted to take their friendship beyond the next level. At least she assumed it meant something. Not that they had time to discuss anything when Kristen almost burst through the door. Her friend had stayed after Eric had reluctantly left.

The thought of him staying made her heart quiver in excitement.

Joy double-checked the kid's table. Everything set and ready to go. She smiled at the memory of Eric's earlier smiley-face arrangement of the cups. He was so cute, creative, and fun.

What would he do now? Would they start

dating?

Or, was all that out of sympathy for her pitiful damsel-in-distress night? Was it just a heat of the moment thing and didn't really mean anything? Maybe she misread the whole thing, and by kissing him sent him running away.

What if he packed up and returned to California, or what if he's wondering how he could let her down easy? He'd probably pat her on the head like a little sister and send her on her way.

How could she have been such an idiot? She shouldn't have kissed him. Not without really knowing what he thought and how he felt.

Joy glanced at the clock on the wall. Bummer. With the kids coming in a few minutes, she didn't have time to dig a hole. One of these days, she'd just burrow in and stay forever, become a cave dweller away from heart issues and real-life stuff where people die and leave.

"Gooooood morning, Joy!" Willamena carried a tray full of juice-filled cups and set them on the worktable. "Our little ones should be arriving soon." She enveloped Joy in a big, squeeze-the-air-out-of-the-lungs hug. "Is there anything else I can do to help?"

"No, I think we're ready." Joy rested for a moment in her great aunt's pressure-filled but healing touch. "We should have twelve kids arriving soon."

Willamena released her and patted Joy's cheek. "Kiddos are always so precious. When my boys were little, they were wide open. If I could have bottled their rambunctiousness, I would be a millionairess."

A mini-bus from the Wee-Ones Daycare, followed by several vehicles pulled into the parking lot outside.

"Looks like our visitors have arrived." Willamena toddled out to meet the group and direct them inside.

Joy's curiosity piqued when she noticed Kristen's neighbor, Brandon. A little girl held his hand as she hopped to the greenhouse door.

Brandon smiled at Joy. "I hoped you would be working today." He nodded toward the little girl with big blue eyes and blonde hair. "This is my niece, Molly."

Joy stooped down to eye level. "Hi Molly, I'm glad you and your friends are here."

"Me too! Teacher said we get to plant flowers." She held up her little fingers. "I'm three."

"Wow, three is a big number."

"Yes. And next birfday I will be four."

"That's really cool, Molly." Joy touched Molly's soft hair. "You ready to start on our project? You get to take home a flower that's already budding and plant a new one too."

"Wow!" Molly's little eyes rounded in awe-struck delight.

Willamena easily maneuvered the kids to sit down.

Brandon leaned toward Joy. "You been doing okay?"

"Yeah." She gave him a curious look. "Everything seems good."

"Good. Could I ask you a question about Kristen?" His expression turned serious. "Is she avoiding me?"

"No, on the contrary. She had to leave town for her job with a new client in Sun Valley."

"Good." He nodded but still seem troubled. "I mean not good that she left, but I wasn't sure if she had just said that so she had an excuse not to go out with me."

"Brandon, she likes you. You don't have anything to worry about."

He nodded again. "Cool. I'm glad. Yeah, that's good. But, she won't be back for a couple of weeks?"

"Probably not. Sounded like a pretty big job."

"Oh." Brandon, his gaze in the distance, rubbed his chin. "That's not good."

"Why isn't that good?"

"Well, I was just hoping you two would be doing some things together. Um. But two weeks, huh? So, are you and Kristen going to do anything together when she returns?"

Joy grinned. "Always."

Brandon smiled and nodded, but still seemed worried. "Good. That's good."

She put her arm around his shoulder. "Kristen does like you."

"Good." He smiled, looked at the ground, smiled bigger, then looked back at her. "That's really good."

~~~~

Eric followed the sound of kid squeals but stopped when he saw Joy touching some guy, putting her arms around his shoulder.

Did he misread everything about last night?

Was Joy in the habit of being affectionate with every guy she met? How could he have allowed his emotions free reign? What a jerk he'd been.

"Eric." Joy's face flamed red as she stepped away from the man. "I'm surprised you're here."

"Obviously." Eric didn't mean to sound that sarcastic.

She cocked her head as she surveyed him. "I mean, I'm glad you're here."

"Yeah, I can tell."

Joy shook her head and stared at the ground for a moment, then looked back at him with eyes narrowed. "Eric. This is Brandon. Kristen's neighbor."

Eric gripped Brandon's hand tight enough to let the guy know he meant business.

"Brandon." Joy continued as she looked at the guy then back at Eric. "This is Kristen's brother, Eric."

Seemingly unaware of Eric's death grip, Brandon gave him an enthusiastic handshake. "Oh hey, it's great to meet you. Kristen thinks the world of you."

Joy took a step toward Eric and whispered. "Brandon asked Kristen out. He was just making sure she wasn't avoiding him."

Eric swallowed hard and attempted a smile. He *had* misread the situation, and from the look on Joy's face, he really screwed up.

Maybe he should pick up a shovel and let her hit him with it. Joy had that look that said she was hurt, miserable, and he was an absolute idiot. He blew out a breath and surveyed the greenhouse ceiling.

~~~~

Joy picked up the large bag of potting soil and turned her attention to the kids. Was Eric upset about Brandon, or upset about last night's kiss and came to let her know they made a mistake?

She should have never let her emotions down, never let her heart out from behind the wall she'd carefully constructed. Life was way too scary. Too many hurts. Too much pain. Too many risks. Plants for the most part were easy. Water, sunshine, soil, and they were happy. People? Way too complex. And men? Who knew?

Willamena's hand rested on Joy's arm. "You might want to back off a touch on the soil."

Joy stopped the flow of potting soil, but not before she had immersed the end of the table in a foot of dirt.

Twelve sets of little eyes surveyed her

with a look of horrified suspicion. "Sorry kids, I should have been paying more attention. It's important to pay attention, isn't it?"

Molly nodded. "My mommy says to always pay tenchun or we might get hit by a car."

One little boy waved his hand. "My mommy rubs her neck a lot because of tenchun."

Joy grinned and glanced at Eric who just happened to be rubbing the back of his neck. He dropped his hand and gave her what she hoped was an apologetic smile.

Half of her wanted to fling dirt at him and the other wanted to vault herself back into his arms.

Eric picked up a small garden trowel and walked next to her. "Need some help?"

"How good are you at cleaning up messes?"

"I guess that depends on whether or not you'll accept my apology. I'll admit it, I was jealous."

"Really?" He was already jealous. Was that good or bad? Her heart said good, her mind flashed danger signals. Oh, good grief ... danger?

She knew the guy since they were kids. He was wonderful. Joy stared into Eric's eyes and so longed to be back in his arms.

Willamena stepped between them. With a

smile, she took them both by the arms and turned them away from the table. "Perhaps you two should remember we have twelve very impressionable children watching your every move."

Warmth radiated Joy's cheeks and by the look of Eric's red face, he felt the same embarrassment.

Eric whirled around and scooped up some soil in his trowel. "Who wants dirt?"

Little hands raised in the air followed by a few squeals.

He shined a grin at Joy as he filled each pot. Eric wasn't exactly neat about the process, but the kids seemed to enjoy his method more than her usual careful, exact, never-spill-a-drop routine.

An hour later, tiny dirty hands gave her hugs and high-fives to Eric. A quick trip to the sink to wash off, and the little ones skipped, hopped, and ran to the waiting bus to return to the day-care.

Eric stood next to her as they waved goodbye. "Well, I understand why you enjoy your kid time. They are definitely entertaining."

Joy chuckled and elbowed his side. "You are the one who was entertaining. We are going to need a fire hose to clean you off. Are you always that dirty when you build your houses?"

He brushed off his shirt and pants sending up a dust cloud. "Okay, I admit to maybe enjoying myself a little too much."

Willamena handed Eric a wet towel. "You are as bad as my boys were when they were little. My late husband used to call them dirt magnets. Or was that dirt maggots?" She patted his shoulder. "But you were great with the kids. They had a wonderful time."

With a turn, she grinned at Joy. "And you, young lady, after you clean up, should come to my house tonight for our quilting group. I've told all the girls about you and they want to meet you."

Joy shot a desperate look at Eric hoping he would suggest something else for the evening. Dinner. A walk on the trails. Even a root canal sounded better than sitting around a quilt group.

She couldn't even sew a button on a dress without needing an infusion for blood loss from needle pricks.

Eric nodded at Joy. "That sounds like a great idea. It'll give you some time away from this place and a great opportunity to meet new people."

She smiled at Willamena but really wanted to cry.

Obviously, Eric didn't want to spend time with her this evening. And to top it off, she would have to be in the company of women she didn't know, and who would expect her to know things like sewing and girl things, and the only thing she knew was how to plant stuff and dig holes.

Willamena hugged Joy with a pop-the-stuffing-out-of-your-body hug. "I'm so glad! You will love the girls and they will love you."

Joy staggered when her aunt released her and grabbed Eric's arm. "I need you to do something for me in the office."

~~~~

Eric walked next to Joy. From the vice grip she had on his arm, he surmised he was in trouble. Not that he was sure why, but at least she was holding onto him.

Joy shut the office door and turned to him. "What are you thinking?"

He wasn't sure if that was a rhetorical question. And, her huffy look just made her all the cuter. "I ..."

"I don't want to go quilting thing. I can't

sew. I can't do any of that frilly, lady stuff."

Joy paced and her arms flew like a helicopter. "And, those ladies will look at me, and know I can't do any of that stuff, and I'll feel awkward and stupid. And, I'll get poked with giant quilting needles, and they'll have to call paramedics because I'll probably be bleeding all over the place."

Part of him wanted to chuckle. Fortunately, his more intelligent side cautioned to tread carefully. Her reaction had to be more than quilting. "You are not awkward and stupid." He took her in his arms, and she buried her face in his chest. "You are graceful, smart, and beautiful."

"Really?" Her voice was muffled in his shirt.

"Yes, Joy Davidson. You are beautiful." If she had any idea how beautiful she really was, she wouldn't have anything to do with someone like him.

Eric tilted her face up to look in her eyes. "I mean that, but this isn't just about quilting. What's wrong?" He held her close, waited, enjoying the smell of her hair, the feel of her in his arms.

She nestled back against his chest but didn't say anything. Her head moved just a touch, and a small whimper escaped. "Do you not want to spend time with me?"

Eric pulled her tighter. "Joy, I always want to be with you." He leaned down, kissed her soft lips. Kissed them over and over ... because if he stopped he might tell her his true feelings, he loved her, always loved her and always would.

~~~~

Joy sat in her car outside Willamena's 1920's tiny home in downtown Boise. Fifteen minutes late for the quilting circle, quills, quails, or whatever you called them.

The last thing she wanted to do was be cooped up inside. She had holes to dig. How could she unwind if she wasn't in the dirt?

Joy took deep breaths. One minute her heart felt like it would explode from happiness, and the next minute like it was trying to pull her ribcage over itself in a protective measure.

Could hearts be schizophrenic?

The time with Eric had been magical, wonderful, and yet made her stomach twist like a pretzel.

Why did she have to show her insecurities every time they spent time together?

The more she was around him, the more vulnerable, and the greater the risk. And ... the more opportunities for the relationship to develop. But, would that cause a budding romance or a withered heart?

Joy took another deep breath and surveyed her aunt's small yard. During the spring and summer months her aunt's house kept a steady stream of people walking by to admire the lush greenery. A few more weeks and flowers would be peeking their heads through her well-trimmed beds.

Her cell phone rang with the familiar ringtone assigned to Willamena. Joy chuckled as she answered. Her aunt stood on the front porch motioning her inside.

Joy waved and gave a thumbs-up. Yes, she was coming. Two more deep breaths and she stepped out of her car. When she reached the sidewalk, Willamena grabbed her hand like she was a little girl and led her inside.

A temporary table stood in the middle of her aunt's living room with a patchwork of material resembling a jigsaw puzzle of multi-colored squares.

The dining room table was covered in various fabrics with a sewing machine on the end. Three women looked up from their projects as her aunt made introductions and gushed over Joy's accomplishments.

"So nice to meet you, Joy." Ellen, an attractive woman with dark hair and a big smile, gave her a firm but very sweet hug. A hug that said she was already liked and accepted.

Annette, a young woman about her own age, stood and gave her a polite handshake. "Nice to meet you, Joy." Annette's English accent made Joy smile.

Sparkling blue eyes faded by years, world-traveler, feisty, Gilda, Willamena's best friend, enveloped her in a big hug. "About time you joined us. You've been missing the fun for months."

Gilda stepped back to look at her. "As beautiful as always. You look just like your mom. She was such a joy, always laughing, loving life, loving your dad, and loving you." Gilda looked up at the ceiling. "I know she's watching and loving you from heaven."

Willamena put a hand to her chest. "She would be so proud of her Joy, just like I am. Now come over here and help me decide my pattern for the next quilt."

Grateful for the distraction from her growing emotions, Joy followed her aunt into the dining room. "I don't know how to do any of this."

"Just think of quilting like patching together flowers of fabric. The stacks here are twelve-inch squares of different designs. We'll sew them together in a pinwheel, kite, diagonal, or other patterns."

"You can stitch in a ditch." Gilda said.

Joy nodded. "Now that's something I can do. Or at least dig or stand in a ditch. The stitch part might be a little more than I can handle."

Willamena placed a hand on her shoulder. "No, sweet one. Stitch in a ditch is something you do if you don't want to complete intricate designs."

Gilda chuckled and took Joy by the hand. "How about we give you a pair of scissors and you can cut out some squares for us."

Joy sat listening to the ladies visit as she cut squares of fabric for the ladies. Cutting was probably busy work for her, but she hoped her work would come in handy for someone at some time.

"I must admit, I barely got the house ready this evening." Willamena spoke up. "I think I have a problem. No, I know have a problem."

The ladies looked up with curious expressions.

Willamena rung her hands. "I've been

thinking of going for help."

"Whatever is going on, you know we are all here for you." Gilda placed a hand on Willamena's shoulder.

"Well, you know I don't like weeds. Not at all." Willamena kept her head down.

"I don't know if that's a problem." Annette snapped her scissors. "I'm prone to use some rather destructive methods when those evil tyrants attack my garden."

"True. They can be evil, but I have a problem. I knew it was bad, but today I found myself on the front lawn of a neighbor's house pulling their weeds. And, I actually weeded at my doctor's office the other day in the front flower bed. I can't stop. When I see a weed, I just can't let it go. I think I need help. I'm thinking of finding a weedaholic group."

Ellen guffawed. "No, no, no, not that. Sweet friend, the kind of weeds you need help with and the kind of group you might find will be very different."

Gilda looked at Ellen with a confused expression, then threw her head back and laughed.

Annette joined in the revelry.

Joy snorted with laughter at the thought of sweet Willamena standing at the doorway of a group asking for help with her weed issue.

"Don't other people have weed problems?" Willamena turned from left to right trying to understand. Then, her expression changed to a look of horror. "Oh, dear. Oh, dear, you are thinking of marijuana. Oh my, I would *never* do that."

She placed her hand over her heart. "That's not the weed I mean. Oh dear. Oh me." She let out a titter of laughter then broke out in a full force laugh that shook every inch of her body.

Gilda shot a glance at Joy. "I bet you thought quilting groups weren't fun?"

Chapter 6

Sunshine warmed the still cool air as Joy and Eric walked along the old wooden boardwalk on Main Street in Idaho City. Joy visualized the early prospectors, pioneers, and settlers coming with their hopes and dreams of fortune as they rode their wagons into the mining town.

She glanced over and smiled at Eric who looked mighty fine in his casual shirt, jeans, and hiking boots. "So, what do you think we'll find?"

Eric shrugged, "I don't think we'll find much of anything." He smiled as he looked her way. "But, I am grateful for the excuse to get you away from work for an afternoon."

Joy did feel like a kid being released early from school. It wasn't often she could tear herself away from the property and being away with him made her want to happy dance.

Eric's expression turned serious, but he

had a glint in his eye. "So, how was the quilting thing you went to the other night? You don't seem to have lost any blood."

Joy smiled at the memory. "No needles were involved, instead the ladies had me cut up squares. Fortunately, I can handle scissors. And, I think I laughed more than I have in years at something that happened with Willamena."

"I knew you'd have fun." He playfully nudged her with his shoulder. "So, what was so funny about your Aunt?"

"Let's just say it had to do with weed." Joy stifled a giggle at Eric's confused expression.

They turned toward the welcome center. As they entered, Joy checked out the small gift shop area. Gasping, she grabbed Eric and pointed. Behind the counter sat a photo of two women of what seemed to be from the 1800's, but the faces were definitely Kristen and Joy. Someone had edited the picture. The caption read, *Idaho's finest Jewels*.

"Well, I wondered when you would come." An older gentleman, stooped with time, stood behind her grinning as he pointed to her and then at the photo.

Unsure if she should respond, she glanced at Eric. He moved closer, his hand protectively resting against her back.

Lisa Buffaloe

The man took down the photo and handed it to her. "I've been looking forward to seeing who you were. Where is your friend?" His kind eyes and smile, put her at ease.

"My friend?" Joy leaned into Eric's protective presence.

The gentleman pointed to Kristen in the picture, "The other young lady."

"Uh, she couldn't come." Joy looked at Eric and wished he would say something. Instead, he seemed riveted to the photo.

"Such a shame, I was hoping to meet both of you." The older man rummaged in a desk drawer and pulled out a card. "This is for you. Can you make sure your friend sees this too? The instructions were implicit." He handed her a computer-generated letter.

Joy held the note in her hand and read,

For two of Idaho's finest Jewels.

Fly on wings of Eagles from riverside to the shore. Swing in to Merrill to find the marker for your next path. In the granite lies your next clue.

"Who left this?" Eric's voice gruff, he stood at full height as he moved in front of Joy.

The man studied Eric, his face curious. "Can't exactly say. Found it in a package on the front porch the other morning. It also had a generous donation to Idaho City's historical district along with these instructions."

A rambunctious family entered the store and beckoned the older gentleman for his help.

Joy fingered the paper. First a fortune cookie with a clue that leads here, and now a photo with her and Kristen leading them forward on another adventure. Who would take the time to do all this and why?

Eric put his hand on her shoulder. "I don't like this, especially since the person thought you two would be alone. You better call Ray."

"I'm definitely going to call Ray. But, maybe it's just a game or something?"

"I don't like anyone playing a game with you or Kristen."

"I thought you wanted me to have fun?" Seeing Eric puffed up and protective made her less cautious and even more curious. "Let's look around and figure out where the next clue leads."

"Fine, but you better stay close." Eric took her hand in his, pulling her closer. "No telling what danger lurks ahead."

If she had been a balloon, she'd have floated above his head. His warm hand, big and rough from working in the building trade, made her feel protected, safe ... loved.

Lisa Buffaloe

They stepped outside into the warm sunshine. An older man and his wife strolled on the boardwalk, peeking in the windows of shops and buildings.

A family piled out of a minivan, the dad playfully shouting, "There's gold in them thar hills."

Joy squeezed his hand and playfully bumped against him. "The danger is overwhelming."

Smiling, Eric gave her a sideways glance. "You never know if they are all part of some diabolical plot."

Joy squeezed his hand. Free as a little girl without a care in the world.

Enjoying the town's history, they visited gift shops, a little museum, had lunch, then drove over to the old pioneer cemetery to see if they could find a gravesite of one of Eric's relatives from the 1800 gold rush days.

Eric took her hand and led her up the hill. "They say there's over 200 hundred grave markers, but only twenty-eight were deaths from natural causes. Idaho City was a wild place during the gold rush. They say there might be more than 2000 graves scattered around the area. No telling how many people roamed this area looking for a chance at fortune."

"That's terrible so many people lost their lives."

"Yeah it is. Some came hoping to make a better life for themselves or their families like he did." Eric stopped next to an old grave marker and pointed. "He was only twenty-five when he was shot over a mining claim. He left a pregnant wife who carried my great grandfather. Man, I can't imagine those who lost their loved ones back then."

"That's so sad." She couldn't imagine how devastated his wife must have been at her young husband's death. Joy glanced around, the air oppressive with sadness. "These old tombstones, they're markers of lives cut short, hopes and dreams dead and buried."

Eric turned toward her, his gaze tender. "I'm sorry. I didn't even think about you and your past. I'm sorry I brought you up here and started talking about stuff like that."

"It's okay." Joy shrugged, wished she could shake off the dark cloud that hovered over her soul.

Eric took her in his arms, held her close against his chest. "I wish I could go back and make it all better. Fix everything for you."

"Me too." She'd dig a hole, but digging here

would definitely be a problem. Safe against his chest was much better anyway. He held her long, tight, but not too tight. She closed her eyes, listened to his heartbeat, slow and steady telling her everything would be alright.

An old car stopped on the road nearby, and an older couple exited. Walking hand-in-hand they talked quietly as they walked among the gravesites.

Eric took Joy's hand and led her to his pickup truck. He opened the door for her, waited until she was buckled in.

He held her close. Fingered her hair. "I really do wish I could fix everything."

Heart moaning, Joy sat still. Wishing, wanting, the past to be renewed, the future to start with a new life to go forward.

He gently shut her door, got in his side, then sat for a moment.

Eric turned toward her, his eyes moist, tender. "I know I can't fix what happened to you. But, the past doesn't have to stop your future."

"I guess time keeps going whether we want it to or not."

"Do you want it to keep going?" His voice soft, pleading.

The question surprised, shocked, made

her think. "Well, yes. Sure. … I mean, definitely, yes."

"Good." Eric readjusted in his seat, turned his head to the ceiling. "Look, I've known you for years. Loved you for years. And, I want to keep loving you." He turned back toward her. "I love you, Joy. I want to make life better for you. I want to…" His voice trailed off and he leaned toward her, kissed her long, hard, yet gentle.

Heart thundering, soaring, flying, skittering. She clung to him. He loved her. *He really loved her.*

But, what if something happened to him? What if she said she loved him and then he left her or died like her parents.

Would God really give her a chance at happiness? She pulled away, her hands hugging her chest.

Eric's gaze searched hers. "Sorry." He turned away, started the truck, and drove out of the town. His hands gripped the steering wheel, his knuckles white. "I'll take you home."

"No. Not yet." She didn't want to go, didn't want to leave things hanging. The promise of love that had been in the air, she didn't want it to go.

"Did you want to check out the next clue?"

His voice flat, hurt.

"No. Eric, you didn't let me talk." She put her hand on his, searched his face. "Please pull over. Give me a chance to say something."

He parked the car on the side of the road. Stared out the front window.

Joy got out of the vehicle, ran to the river, stopped and leaned against a crooked and bent tree next to the rushing water. *God, help me. Would you be kind enough to give me what I want? Oh God, help me. Fix me*. Tears came, she couldn't stop them. So tired of living in the past, tired of running, so wanting to move forward. Sobs bent her over. Washing, cleansing.

Eric stood behind her, rubbed her back. "I'm sorry, Joy. I never ever want to hurt you."

"I'm scared. I'm so scared."

Through her watery gaze, she stared at the ground. The puddle of her tears slowly absorbed into the earth. "God took away everyone I loved." She shuddered. "The only memories I have of my parents are in photos and videos. I don't want them to fade away."

"I'm sorry." Eric's voice soft, compassionate.

The words in her mind searched for an exit. Thinking them was scary enough, saying them even scarier. Joy took a deep breath, tried to compose herself. "If I say I love you, will I lose you too?"

"Oh, Joy. You won't ever lose me." His voice spoke into her ear, tender, melting her.

Knees weak, Joy steadied herself against the tree.

His hand rested against her back. "What happened to you was awful. Nothing I can say or do will replace what you lost. Your parent's death was tragic and terrible. But, I love you and I want to be with you forever."

"Joy, do you love me?" Eric's tender voice, whispered beside her.

The longing in his voice cut deep into her quivering scared, unsure heart so wanting love. If she said she loved him out loud what would happen?

Would something terrible start in motion, a break in the cosmos that would shatter her heart again and leave her in a dark hole with no way out? Or, dare she hope the words would start something exciting and new?

Oh God, show me a sign.

~~~~

Heart breaking, Eric stood next to Joy.

A quiet whimpering moan came deep from within her as she sank to her knees.

Eric knelt beside her. His prayers, desperate for her healing, cried out for help, for an opportunity to make a new life with her. Would she, and her heart, take a chance on him?

He wanted to be her knight in shining armor, the one who rescues the damsel in distress. Even with his tainted armor and human failures, would God give him a chance?

Would God allow him to love someone as precious as Joy? *Please, God.*

Other than an occasional shudder, she didn't move. A slight wind blew through the trees, gently swaying her hair around her face.

Maybe he shouldn't have pushed, maybe he shouldn't have said what he did.

Eric got off his knees and sat next to her. He'd wait. For however long it took, he'd wait for Joy.

Without a word, she readjusted and sat next to him. Time stood still, waited. Nothing else mattered. He'd wait.

Joy picked up a rock and gasped.

He leaned forward to see her holding a smooth stone in the shape of a heart.

Her thumb played across the surface as she

turned it over and over. Gazing upward, the tears still pooling in her beautiful eyes. She held the stone close against her chest. Again, she moaned.

~~~~

Joy held the rock against her chest. Her heart had been hard as stone for so long. She didn't want to live like this forever. Didn't want to miss a chance at love, but how do you melt a stone heart?

How do you let go of all the hurt and pain?

The verse came to mind, *I will give you a new heart and put a new spirit in you; I will remove from you your heart of stone and give you a heart of flesh.*

A flesh heart hurts. Did she want that? Then again, didn't her walled-off heart bring pain?

All she did was feel pain, the more she tried to keep her heart from being hurt, the more her heart hurt.

Maybe letting her heart melt with love would actually cure her heart hurts?

Joy screamed in her soul and kicked the dirt with her shoe. Was there any way to win? Any way to not hurt?

Lisa Buffaloe

Eric was safe, but he was human, and people died and left and could bring pain.

Standing to her feet, she motioned with her hand for Eric to sit and wait.

Unable to dig a hole and hide, Joy ran along the side of the river, running as far as she could to release tension. Running to hide, running from herself, running, needing to outrun the doubts and fears that hunted and haunted her.

Breathless, she stopped where a fallen tree blocked her path. She didn't want to go on, didn't want to live like this forever. She wanted to change, needed to change.

Looking at the stone heart in her hand, the sobs came again. "I'm so afraid, God. How do I let go?"

A small voice spoke in the inner depths of her heart. *Trust.*

She knew, knew in her soul, but hated to admit it even to herself. Her fears weren't only about people.

Could she trust God again? Trust Him not to take away those she loved?

Sobbing, Joy looked up, beyond the trees. "I want a love that lasts forever. I don't want to lose again those I love. Please, I don't want to hurt anymore."

An eagle came into view, gliding on air

currents. He didn't even need to flap, the wind blew him, he flew free. No limits. Unbridled floating on air.

Oh, how she wanted to fly free. Free from earthly confines, earthly concerns, and earthly pain.

Again, the quiet voice spoke, *Trust Me. Trust My unfailing, eternal love. I won't ever leave you.*

"God, you didn't protect me." As soon as she said those words, she felt a pain, a sorrow, that came from within her yet from outside her.

It wasn't true, she knew it wasn't true. She lost her parents, yet God was always with her. He never left her.

Oh, God.

Joy sank to the ground as Bible verses came to mind. *I am a Father to the fatherless. God places the lonely in families. I will never leave you or forsake you.*

Images flashed in her mind. Aunts, uncles, grandparents, friends, her church, employees at the garden center, Eric, Kristen and their family, all had been there for her.

Had she stared so long, so hard, at what she missed, that she missed everything around her?

She grasped the stone heart, held it aloft and opened her hand. It was all she had to offer.

Lisa Buffaloe

All she had to give.

"It's yours God. I want a heart of flesh. Forgive me for running from you. Please make me whole. I'm ready."

Joy placed the rock on the fallen tree.

Tears came once again, but these tears were different, they washed, cleansed, released.

Through blurry, bleary eyes, she again glanced upward. The Eagle flew straight up, straight up toward the sun, straight up beyond her sight.

Chapter 7

Eric stood, watching, praying, pacing. Should he go after Joy? Should he go look for her or give her space?

He kicked the dirt, kicked trees, threw rocks, paced back and forth, sat by the river, walked by the river, prayed by the river. He waited until the shadows grew long, until he thought he would go crazy.

When he couldn't stand it anymore, he walked, following the river, praying Joy was okay, praying her heart would trust him, praying God would give them both a chance.

An eagle flew overhead, gliding on air currents. Man, he wished he could grab a ride and fly to see if Joy was okay.

He hurried his pace, searching ahead, occasionally glancing up to watch the eagle.

What was that verse about eagles? Something about waiting on God? He remembered the verse, but really didn't want to have to wait anymore for Joy.

He was ready to settle down, ready to take her home with him. Then again, was the verse waiting on God or hoping on God? Maybe both based on the translation.

The eagle soared higher, soared toward the sun and out of his sight. Eric smiled and picked up his pace to a run. "Okay God, I'll wait and I'll hope I don't have to wait any longer. I'll take good care of her if you'll let me."

Eric kept running, further and further with no sign of Joy. He kicked into high gear, desperate to find her, desperate to hold her in his arms and keep her safe.

~~~~

Joy wiped her eyes, looked around. The sun hung low on the horizon. A cool wind cut through her light jacket. How far had she run?

Eric. Oh no.

He must be worried sick or think she'd gone crazy.

She turned and ran back to him, running on tired but refreshed legs.

Ahead, something crashed through the brush. Heart racing, praying for protection, Joy ducked low behind a big rock.

The footsteps pounded past, running and bashing. Maybe it was a bear or a moose? She waited until it passed, then turned to run to the safety of Eric's arms. She should have stayed where she could see Eric. Stayed where she would be safe. She didn't want to be without him ever again. She needed him.

Now that her heart was squishy and not stony, she needed someone to protect her heart. She needed Eric. Okay, she needed God. But she hoped God would give her Eric.

When did the woods get so dark? Joy stopped and caught her breath. Was she running the right way? Yes, she had run by the river, so her direction was correct, but had she run this far?

What if she had passed Eric and he had gone somewhere else, what if he left her, what if he didn't wait? He would wait, wouldn't he?

She stifled a scream as she ran. Forget not calling. She needed him. "Eric!" She yelled over and over and over. She had to find him.

She had to get back with him. Didn't ever want to leave him. She ran faster. "Eric!"

~~~~

Eric screeched to a halt in front of a fallen

tree. Joy's rock sat on the top. She had been here. He grabbed the rock, held it close. The river to his right moved fast, swollen against its banks. He shuddered, squelched the fearful thought rising in his mind.

The trail ended here, did she turn back, go another way, was there a trail he missed?

Desperate, crazy wild, heart pounding like a wild man, he wiped the sweat from his forehead and turned to run back.

What if whoever left that note in Idaho City had been watching for Joy? Maybe she got kidnapped. "God, please help me find her!"

Limbs grabbed at his face, his clothes, as he ran. He cupped his hands to his mouth. "Joy!"

"God, help me find Joy."

"Joy!" He yelled again. Faster and faster he ran, tripping, crashing through the underbrush, looking, watching for side trails, watching for any sign of her.

Whomp!

Eric groaned as he sat up and blinked to get the dirt from his eyes. Warm sticky fluid ran from his nose.

Reaching up, he pulled back to find blood on his fingers.

He didn't have time for this. He must have tripped over a rock.

Blood gushed from what felt like a broken nose. As he tried to clear his head, he wiped off as much blood as he could and held his nose closed to try and stop the flow.

He had to find Joy.

Head pounding, nose feeling like it would fall off his face, he kept running.

Then he heard her, she was calling. No sound had ever been sweeter than her voice. But, the voice wasn't light, she was afraid. He dug deep to find the speed he needed. He'd rip apart anyone who tried to hurt her. Rip them limb to limb, not leave a trace, he'd....

Her scream screeched him to a halt. She stood down the path from him, her eyes wide, teary, horrified.

Oh, God, what if someone hurt her.

~~~~

Joy almost fell over she stopped so fast. She couldn't help but scream when she saw Eric with blood running down his face.

Did he get attacked by a bear?

Sobbing, she ran to him and buried her face in his bloody shirt. "Are you okay? Are you okay? "Oh, please tell me you're okay."

"I'm okay." Eric enveloped her in his arms.

Desperate, tight, holding her close. "Are you okay? Please tell me you're okay."

"I'm okay, too. I am, I really am. What happened? Did something attack you?"

"No, no. I'm okay. Just fell."

She clung to him. His heart pounded hard against his chest. Pounded hard and deep. Safe, he was safe, she was safe, they were safe. She sent up a prayer thanking God.

"I'm so grateful you're okay." He held her close as his heart fell back to a normal pace. Their hearts seemed to beat in unison now, steady, slower.

She adjusted to look up at his beautiful eyes. Even though they were a little bloodshot, maybe even a little black around his eyes. "You don't look good." She grabbed a tissue from her jacket pocket and wiped his bloody nose.

Eric's nose seemed to tilt a little to the left. "Oh no, you really got hurt."

"I was looking for you. I was so afraid something happened to you." He pulled her back against his chest.

"I'm so sorry. I didn't mean to worry you. I just needed some time alone. Forgive me?"

"No need to ask for forgiveness." He dipped his head, caught her gaze. "I'm just glad you are okay."

"I really am okay. And, I mean that in more than just the physical sense."

Eric smiled, curious. "Really?"

Joy returned his smile. "Yes, really. Now, will you do me a favor?

His tender eyes surveyed her. "Anything for you."

"Kiss me?"

His kiss sent her toes tingling, her stomach doing happy somersaults, and her soul soaring.

She nestled against his chest. "Eric?"

"Yes."

Joy took a deep breath, took the chance. "I love you."

He jerked back, joy in his gaze. "You said it! You do? Really?"

"Yes, I love you."

"I love you too!" Eric kissed her over and over and over.

Chuckling, Joy staggered back. Surely her lips were swollen by the time they stopped kissing. "It's getting dark."

"Well, will you look at that?" Goofy smiling, he glanced around with a dazed expression.

"Marry me." Eric got down on one knee. "Marry me. I don't have a ring yet, but I'll get one, a big one, whatever you want. I promise to

Lisa Buffaloe

be with you, there for you, through the good and bad, through the hole digging days."

"What?" *Marriage*? Joy blinked, looked at him. Her heart went into overdrive. Was this what happened when you let your heart out to play, when the stone melted? Would God really let her have love and get married? "Isn't this too fast?"

Eric took her hand in his. "Why? We're adults, we've known each other forever. You know my family and they all love you. Marry me."

"Aren't we supposed to wait until we date a long time?" The wind grew in intensity, the shadows darkening. Joy shivered.

Chuckling, Eric rubbed her arms, pulled her close. "I don't think there's a time limit on that sort of thing. We have now. We're old enough. Marry me. I'll marry you right now or wait until you plan a big wedding. Whatever you want. I want to take care of you, love you forever. I want to fall asleep with you in my arms, wake up to you in the mornings. I won't ever leave you. Come on, let's get to the car where you can be warm." He took her hand and led her to the car, opened the door for her.

Joy sat down, waited until he got in his side and started his vehicle. "I love you, but I don't think I can."

~ ~ ~ ~

Eric's heart lurched. "What do you mean? I don't understand. If we love each other, why wouldn't we get married?"

She shook her head. "No, it's not that." Her gaze locked with his. Her eyes tender, loving, yet something else there, something he didn't understand.

Tears welled as she continued. "I want to marry you, but I think I have to wait several years."

"What? Why?"

Joy took a deep breath, blew it out, her gaze turned toward the front window. "Well, I've been mad at God for most of my life for taking my parents. And, I finally just now make peace with him so he probably wants me to make penance or something. I'll probably need to be really good for several years before he'll let me be happy with you."

Eric sat still, wondering where Joy's line of reasoning came from, wondering how to respond. Part of him wanted to smile at her response, but her seriousness dampened his mood cautioning him to be careful with her heart. Praying for wisdom, Eric turned up the heater and drove out onto the road.

Joy kept her head down. "I really do love you."

"I really love you too."

They rode on in silence. His headlights the only beam of light on the dark road. His heart ached.

How could he help Joy understand his love and God's love? They both wanted the best for her. Not that Eric was a prize, but he did love her and would try and make her the best husband he could.

He kept his hands on the wheel, praying for guidance on what he felt he should say.

A memory returned. Eric kept his eyes on the road and prayed this would help Joy understand. "Remember when I came back from California? Remember the big party my parents had for me?

"Yes, that was really sweet. They were all so glad you were back home." She smiled and leaned her head against the headrest. "I was too."

He grinned at her response. "Boy, that made me feel so good to have all of you there welcoming me home." He paused for a moment. "Did you know my dad really didn't want me to go to California?"

"I didn't know that."

"Yeah, he wanted me to learn the building techniques from him, not someone else. But, I was pretty stubborn and went on without his blessing. All those years I knew he preferred me home with him, working with him, and for him."

"He never showed his disappointment, always said the sweetest things about you." Joy said. "He still does."

"He's a neat man. I'm grateful I have him for my dad. And, I'm grateful he always welcomed me home."

"Your dad would have welcomed you home no matter where you had gone or what you had done."

"Yep. Just think, he's just a man. How do you think God feels when his kids come home?"

~~~~

Joy sunk back in her seat. She had never thought about that, thought about how God feels when his kids finally come home.

Then again, she knew the story of the prodigal son, the one who took his inheritance

Lisa Buffaloe

and left his dad. Left his dad, partied, lost everything, even found himself working in a pig pen he was so broke.

But, when the young man came home, his dad came running, threw him a party and welcomed him home without a word of condemnation. No penance was needed, no repayment expected.

Really? That easy? That beautiful? That loving? Really? A warming deep in her soul, deep in her heart, enveloped her. "How could God love us that much?"

Eric smiled, his eyes twinkling as he turned toward her. "Because he is God, he is love, he loves his children, and his grace is amazing."

Joy sat there, smiling, smiling probably as goofy as Eric smiled earlier.

Why didn't she know this earlier? Maybe she did, maybe it was always there but her anger and hurt never let her see the truth. "It's really too good to be true, you know?"

"Yes, it is. God is good. He is true and he is good, really good, super-good, amazing good. Joy, he loves you and so do I."

She relaxed into her seat. Considered. Marveled. "It's really a wow thing, don't you think?"

He chuckled. "It *really* is a wow thing."

How could God love that much? How could he love the wanderers, the lost, the hurt, the angry? Amazing. Wonderful. God's love, a love that doesn't let go, a love that welcomes home, a love that will allow her to love. "Does your offer still stand?"

"If you mean the offer to marry you, I'll pull over the next chapel we find and marry you right now if you'll let me."

"Eric, I would love to be your wife. Yes!"

He stomped on the brakes, jerked the car to the side of the road. "*Really?*"

She nodded. Smiled wide at his wide smile. She sat back dazed, happy dazed, ecstatic dazed. She was going to be Mrs. Eric West.

He fist-pumped the air, then reached over and took her in his arms, held her close. "I love you, Joy."

"I love you too."

Lisa Buffaloe

Chapter 8

"Coif? What kind of word is that?" Joy couldn't stop giggling as Kristen tried valiantly to get Joy's hair under control.

"I'm going to coif more than your hair if you don't sit still. I want you looking beautiful when you marry my brother. Besides that, you are a gorgeous woman, and I want the photos to show you off. Those wedding pictures last a lifetime you know."

Joy still couldn't believe the turn of events, the joy she felt at what God had given her and was now giving her. Who knew a fun clue would lead her on a heart healing adventure? God did.

"Is Brandon here yet?"

"Yes, he is, and he's looking so good, so very good. I still can't believe he was creative enough to put together the fortune cookie and photo at Idaho City."

Kristen's gaze went dreamy. "That man has

come creative ideas. The next clue led to my first date with him. He's still embarrassed I hadn't been here when you started on the adventure."

"Please thank him again. Brandon might have intended his fortune cookie send us on a direction for you to find him, but God blessed me with a redirection to find God's love and healing." Joy grinned at the memory. "I hope we get to spend more time with Brandon in the future."

"Girlfriend, if I have my way, I hope we all spend a lifetime together. Brandon is a keeper, and I want to keep that man with me forever. I wonder if I should ask him for his hand in marriage?"

"Ha, you probably would. Should I be looking for a ring soon?"

"I certainly hope so. If it's half as nice as the one my brother gave you, I'd be a happy woman."

Joy smiled as she looked at her custom-made, custom-designed heart-shaped ring Eric had given her for their engagement. Perfect, just perfect, like him.

Kristen handed Joy a mirror to check her hair.

Joy gasped at the sight of herself. "Wow. I

didn't know my hair could do that?"

Kristen smiled. "I've been wanting to make you up since we got old enough to wear makeup. You just didn't know what could be brought out with a little makeup and hair dressing, did you?"

"I didn't." Joy stood, smoothed out her wedding dress and surveyed herself in the full-length mirror. Her silk dress, beautiful, simple, elegant, the one her mom had worn when she married her dad. The perfect fit felt like she'd been enveloped in a hug from her mom.

She glanced heavenward, whispered a prayer for God to tell her Mom and Dad hello and asked God if it would be okay that they could see her happy. Somehow, she knew God in his goodness would let them see, let them know she was happy.

Kristen hugged her. "I don't know where you are with your thoughts, but I love seeing you smile."

Joy blinked back the happy tears. "I really am happy. I really am." She glanced back in the mirror. "What if Eric wants me to look like this all the time?"

Kristen laughed. "He's going to drool when he sees you. Don't worry, he loves you in your messy state and in your dressy state. You look good no matter what you do. Even when you're digging holes."

Joy picked up the flower arrangement she had chosen to carry down the aisle.

She couldn't believe the time had finally come. Not that they waited very long.

A knock on the door drew their attention.

Willamena burst in the room. Her pink chiffon dress making her look like a giant buff-puff. "Oh, oh, oh, you look so gorgeous!" Willamena hugged her.

Joy gasped for air.

Her aunt released her and stepped back. "Let me look at you. Just, let me look at you. Oh, your mom and dad are dancing in heaven. Just dancing. They loved to dance together. Did I ever tell you that? Your parents had so much fun together and so much fun with you. That's why they named you Joy."

Willamena swayed as though to a silent beat. "They had joy, and then your birth brought them joy. Oh, so much joy. I pray you and Eric do the same. Oh, such good fortune God brought you together. Such joy. Joy, joy, joy. Joy for Joy and Joy for Eric. I've got that joy, joy, joy, joy, down in my heart, down in my heart..." Still singing, she left the room.

Kristen laughed and hugged Joy. "Well,

friend, and soon to be sister, let's get this show on the road. The joy is coming and the joy is just beginning."

Bursting with joy, Joy walked down the aisle where Eric and her new life waited.

The End

The Fortune clues

For those in the Boise area curious to find the clues. For those unable to travel to the Boise area, a photo of the clue marker is found at the end of the author's book page for *The Fortune* (https://lisabuffaloe.com).

1. *Fortune waits* 43.8262 N, 115.8325 W
2. *Fly on wings of Eagles from riverside to the shore. Swing in to Merrill to find the marker for your path. On granite, the question waits.*
Line 8, word 2, letter 4.
Line 8, word 2, letter 3.
Line 8, word 5, letter 5.
Line 8, word 2, letter 5.
Line 8, word 4, letter 3.
Line 8, word 1, letter 1.

Line 1 word 2, letter 5.
Line 2, word 1, letter 2.
Line 1, word 1, letter 4.
Line 1, word 1, letter 4.

Line 1, word 2, letter 7.
Line 2, word 2, letter 1.
Line 4, word 3, letter 3.

Line 1, word 1, letter 3.
Line 2, word 2, letter 1

Line 2, word 2, letter 2.
Line 4, word 2, letter 3.
Line 1, word 2, letter 3

Line 1, word 2, letter 5.
Line 2, word 1, letter 2.
Line 1, word 2, letter 3.
Line 1, word 2, letter 4.

Line 1, word 3, letter 6.
Line 1, word 3, letter 5.
?
Line 1, word 1, letter 4.
Line 4, word 3, letter 2.
Line 7, word 1, letter 4.
Line 3, word 1, letter 5.

Line 6, word 2, letter 1.
Line 6, word 4, letter 3.
Line 6, word 1, letter 3.
Line 6, word 1, letter 4.
Line 6, word 4, letter 4.
Line 6, word 4, letter 2.
Line 6, word 1, letter 4.

About the author

Lisa Buffaloe is an author, gardener, dirt digger, and fortune cookie eater. Her adventurous past experiences bless her with a backdrop to share the beauty and healing growth found when we place our fortunes in God's hands.

Please visit Lisa at...
https://lisabuffaloe.com

Books by Lisa Buffaloe
(Updated July 2023)

Fiction

The Masterpiece Beneath
Nadia's Hope (Hope and Grace Series, 1)
  Prodigal Nights (Hope and Grace Series, 2)
  Writing Her Heart (Hope and Grace Series, 3)
  The Discovery Chapter (Hope and Grace Series, 4)
  Open Lens (Hope and Grace Series, 5)
The Fortune
Grace for the Char-Baked

Non-Fiction

Float by Faith
Heart and Soul Medication
Time with The Timeless One
The Forgotten Resting Place
Present in His Presence
We Were Meant for Paradise
One Lit Step: Devotions for your journey
The Unnamed Devotional
Flying on His Wings
Unfailing Treasures
No Wound Too Deep for The Deep Love of Christ
Living Joyfully Free Devotional, (Volume 1)
Living Joyfully Free Devotional, (Volume 2)

Comforting verses

Perhaps, like Joy, you have lost loved ones. May you find comfort in God's word.

"God places the lonely in families; he sets the prisoners free and gives them joy..." ~ Psalm 68:6 (NLT)

"A father to the fatherless, a defender of widows, is God in his holy dwelling." ~ Psalm 68:5 (NIV)

"He ensures that orphans and widows receive justice. He shows love to the foreigners living among you and gives them food and clothing." ~ Deuteronomy 10:18 (NLT)

"I will not leave you as orphans; I will come to you." ~ John 14:18 (NIV)

"I will give you a new heart and put a new spirit in you; I will remove from you your heart of stone and give you a heart of flesh." ~ Ezekiel 36:26 (NIV)

"Be strong and courageous. Do not be afraid or terrified because of them, for the Lord your God goes with you; he will never leave you nor forsake you." ~ Deuteronomy 31:6 (NIV)

"Those who wait for the Lord [who expect, look for, and hope in Him] will gain new strength and renew their power; they will lift up their wings [and rise up close to God] like eagles [rising toward the sun]; they will run and not become weary, they will walk and not grow tired." ~ Isaiah 40:31 (AMP)

"Listen, dear friends, to God's truth, bend your ears to what I tell you. I'm chewing on the morsel of a proverb; I'll let you in on the sweet old truths, stories we heard from our fathers, counsel we learned at our mother's knee. We're not keeping this to ourselves, we're passing it along to the next generation—God's fame and fortune, the marvelous things he has done." ~ Psalm 78:1-4 (MSG)

Lisa Buffaloe

Thank you for reading
The Fortune

Lisa Buffaloe